GOOD NIGHT, TRILOBITE

BY STEVE VANLANDINGHAM
ILLUSTRATED BY SHANDA WILLIS McDONALD

Good Night, Trilobite
© Copyright 2017 by White Dog Press

All rights reserved. No part of this book may be reproduced or utilized in any form or by any means, electronic or mechanical, including photocopying or recording, by any information or retrieval system, without permission of Chickasaw Press.

ISBN: 978-1-935684-59-6

Book & Cover Design: Gentry Fisher

White Dog Press
c/o Chickasaw Press
PO Box 1548
Ada, Oklahoma 74821

chickasawpress.com

To fossil hunters and fossil lovers, young and old.

"There will be no end to what can be discovered in the rocks."
- Richard Fortey

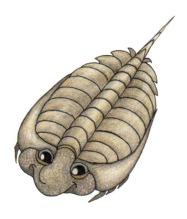

Trilobites were animals that lived in the oceans during the Paleozoic era, long before dinosaurs roamed the earth. They were distant relatives of insects, crabs, and spiders. Trilobites died out at the end of the Paleozoic era, but their fossil remains are found all over the world. The Chickasaw Nation, in south central Oklahoma, is home to rich trilobite fossil deposits. Scientists and fossil hunters travel here from around the world to find and study fossils. This is the story of a trilobite and his friends who lived on the sea floor of what would one day be the Chickasaw Nation.

Once upon a time, long ago, right where we are standing, the land was a sea. It was part of an ocean that covered most of the earth.

In that ancient ocean, some 400 million years ago, there lived a young trilobite. He was sort of a Paleozoic water bug, and his name was Tony.

His scientific name was *Huntonia oklahomae*, which means, "Tony from Oklahoma."

OKHATA'
OCEAN

Tony and his very good friends, Becky the brachiopod and Bryan the bryozoan, were always being chased by their not-so-good friend, Seth the cephalopod, who was always trying to eat them up!

INK<u>A</u>NA'	IMPA
FRIENDS	EAT

Becky the brachiopod

Bryan the bryozoan

Seth the cephalopod

Tony and his friends lived in a time called the Devonian period, when the world was a much different place, full of strange and wonderful creatures. Close your eyes and imagine yourself in the warm waters of a shallow sea, swimming above the ocean floor.

You might see Tony and his friends hanging out, looking for food, or letting food come to them.

YOPI
To Swim

Brachiopods like Becky could open their shells and catch food as it floated by.

Bryan the bryozoan had food-gathering tentacles that could extend out of the holes in his branch-like skeleton.

Tony the trilobite liked to crawl around on the ocean floor and scavenge for leftovers or dig for food in the soft mud.

IMPA'	KOLLI
Food	Dig

Tony had eyes in the back of his head, so he was the first to see Seth trying to sneak up on them.

Ishkin	Ishkobo'
Eyes	Head

The giant cephalopod was lurking above them. He was huge, and he looked hungry!

Hopoba
Hungry

His strong tentacles had sticky suction cups that could grab anything and everything he wanted to eat.

TASHANKCHI'
TENTACLES

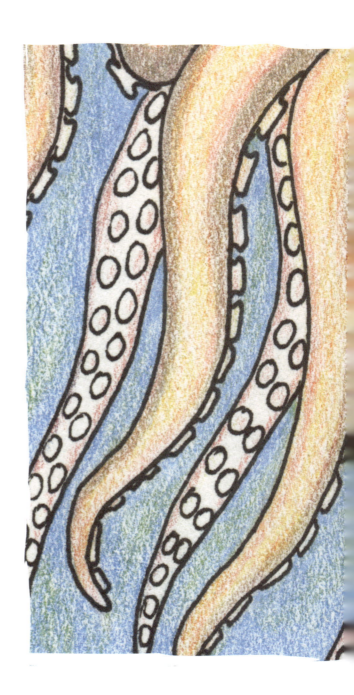

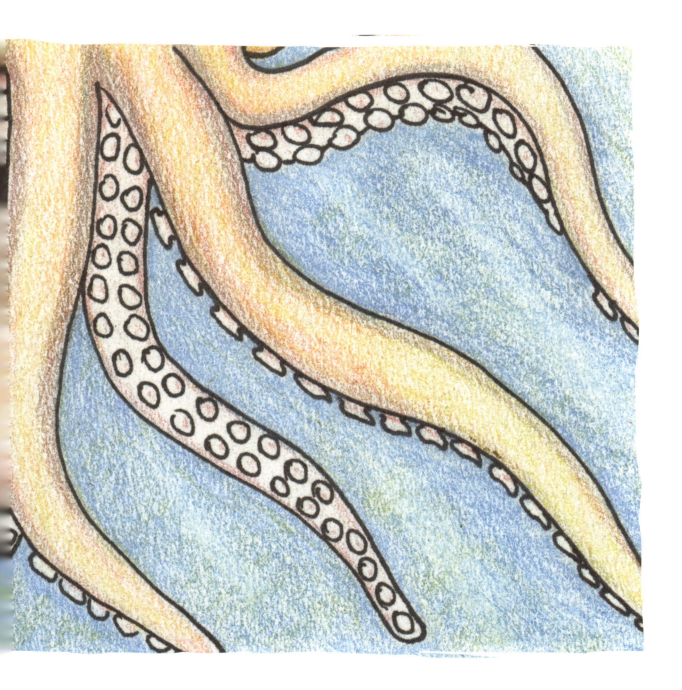

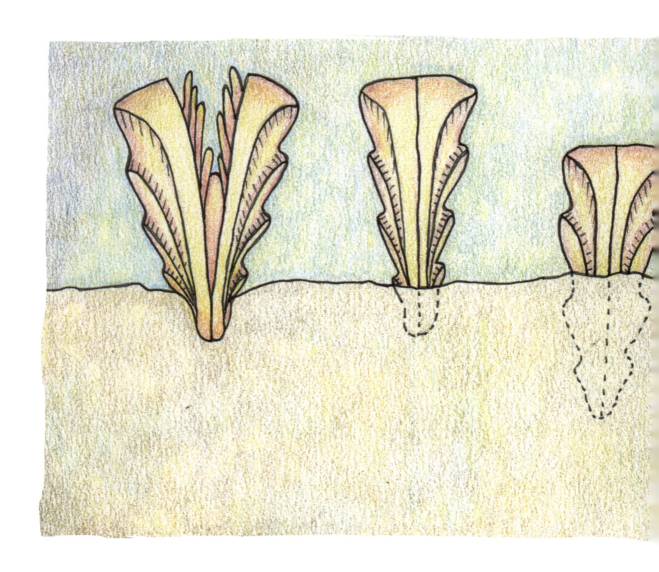

Becky wasn't afraid. She could hide in her shell and burrow down in the sand.

Inokshopa
Afraid

Lohmi
Hide

Shinok
Sand

Bryan could retract his tentacles into their hard, hollow branches, offering a very unappetizing picture to a hungry cephalopod.

Tony had a hard shell, too. But underneath his shell, he had legs and a soft underbelly that would make a tasty snack for Seth.

Iyyi'	Ittakoba'
Legs	Belly

The shadow over Tony became larger and larger. The huge cephalopod was closing in on his meal.

Tony scurried across the ocean floor as fast as his little legs could carry him! But he was too slow to escape from Seth.

PALHKI
Fast

SALAA'SI
Slow

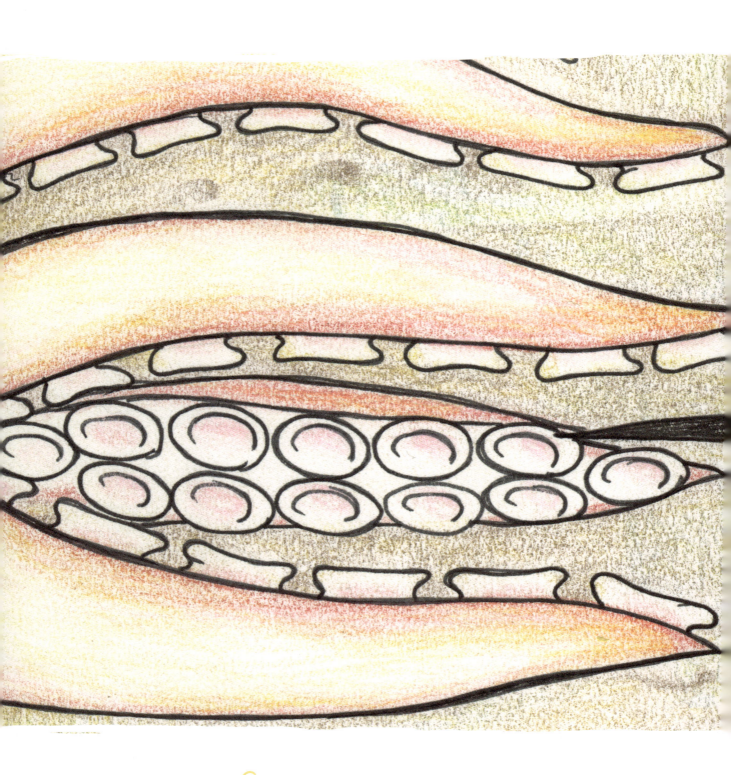

Seth swam closer and closer.

Tony was in trilobite trouble!

At the last second, he began to roll up. Like a roly-poly, he rolled into a tight ball, with plates of armor protecting his soft underbelly.

TO'WA'
BALL

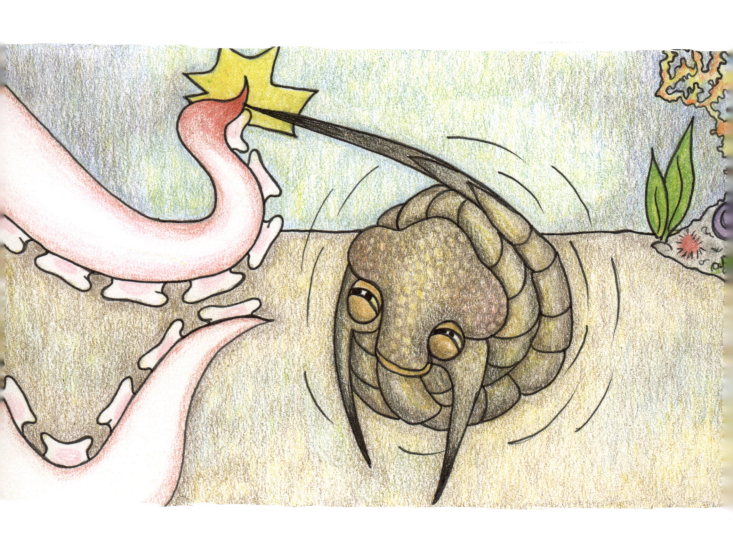

A spine on Tony's tail stuck straight out.
It poked the tip of Seth's soft tentacle.

BAAFA
POKE

Seth paused above his would-be prey, puzzled as to what had suddenly become of his tasty treat.

All he saw was a hard ball with sharp spikes. Ouch!

Naachampoli'	**Alii**
Treat	Ouch

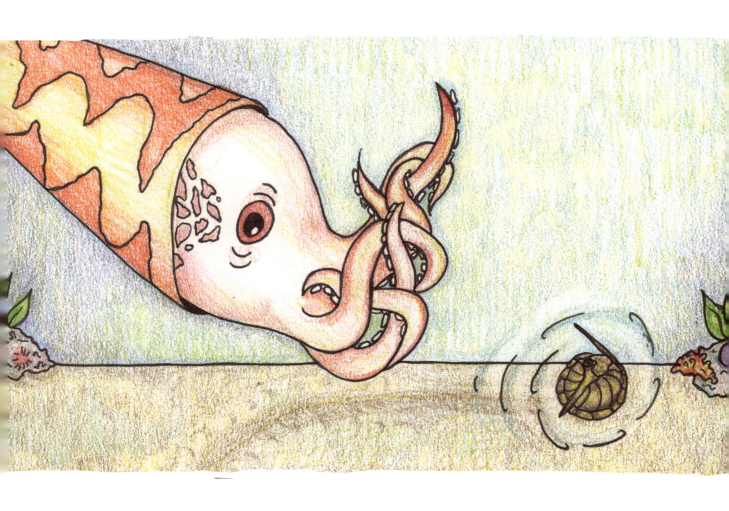

Time to move on, thought Seth.

He shot a jet of water from his built-in funnel and sped off in search of easier pickings.

Oka'
Water

Tony let out a sigh of relief. He was safe for now, and so were his friends.

Perhaps a little nap would be just the thing after all this excitement.

Nosi
Nap

Good night, trilobite, sleep tight. I tucked you into your bed last night. Keep dreaming on, through time and tide. I'll see you on extinction's other side.

Oklhili Chokma
Good Night

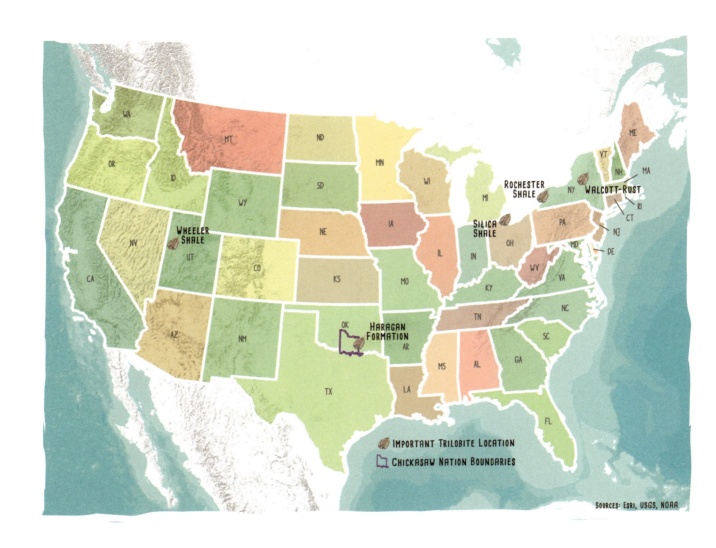

Tony's tale was inspired by a visit to a famous fossil site called White Mound in the Arbuckle Mountains of Oklahoma. Every year hundreds of students from the University of Oklahoma and elementary schools from all over the state come there to search for trilobites, brachiopods, and more. There is probably a fossil site somewhere near you!

TRILOBITE SONG

BY STEVE VANLANDINGHAM

```
C            G         F            C
```
Tony was a trilobite. He lived in the olden days,
```
C            G.        F            C
```
back when Oklahoma lay underneath the waves.
```
Dm           G          Dm           G
```
He crawled on the ocean floor. He rolled into a ball.
```
C            G.        F            C
```
Now he's just a fossil, but he's loved by one and all.

Good night, trilobite. I hope you sleep tight.
400 million years since they turned out the lights.
Let the Silurian seas roll on.
I'll see you in a Devonian dawn.
And it's good night, trilobite, sleep tight.

Becky was a brachiopod. She lived in a Devonian sea,
long before the dinosaurs, or even you or me.
Well, she was a friend of Tony, that trilobite of fame,
and Bryan the bryozoan, you also know his name.

Bye bye, brachiopod, sleep tight in your shell.
So long, bryozoan, sweet dreams to you as well.
I tucked you into your bed last night,
your bed of stone beneath the stars.
And it's good night, trilobite, I hope you sleep tight.

Now Seth, he was a cephalopod. He really liked to eat,
and trilobites and brachiopods, they were his favorite meat.
He was a naughty nautiloid, with mischief on his mind,
always causing trouble of the invertebrate kind.

And it's so long, Seth. I won't say good night,
but I hope all your little friends, they are still sleeping tight.
Well, I tucked you into your bed last night,
your bed of stone beneath the stars.
And it's good night trilobite, sleep tight.

To download "Trilobite Song,"
scan this QR code or go to
chickasawpress.com.

GLOSSARY

Becky the brachiopod

ancient (AYN-shunt):
very old.

brachiopod (BRACK-e-uh-pod):
from the Greek, meaning "arm-foot." A sea animal that has a hard upper and lower shell, similar to a clam.

bryozoan (BRY-uh-zo-uhn):
from the Greek, meaning "moss-animal." An invertebrate animal that lives in colonies, similar to a coral.

cephalopod (SEFF-uh-luh-pod):
from the Greek, meaning "head-foot." A sea animal with tentacles attached to its head, like a squid or octopus.

Devonian (DEE-vohn-e-uhn):
a time period in the Paleozoic era, lasting from 416 to 360 million years ago.

extinct (ek-STINGKT):
no longer in existence.

Tony the trilobite

fossils (FOSS-uhls):
  remains of ancient plants or animals preserved in rock.

invertebrate (in-VER-tuh-bret):
  an animal lacking a backbone.

nautiloid (NAW-tuh-loid):
  any of a group of mostly extinct cephalopods.

Paleozoic (PAY-lee-uh-zo-ick):
  from the Greek, meaning "ancient-life." A time period that lasted from 542 to 250 million years ago.

Silurian (Sil-UR-ee-uhn):
  a time period in the Paleozoic era, lasting from 444 to 416 million years ago.

siphuncle (SY-funk-uhl):
  a tube or siphon in the body of a cephalopod.

tentacles (TEN-tuh-kuhls):
  long, flexible limbs on some animals.

trilobite (TRY-lo-bite):
  a "three-lobed" invertebrate animal, now extinct.

CHICKASAW VOCABULARY

Tashankchi' — Tentacles

English	Chickasaw	Pronunciation
afraid	inokshopa	ehn-nuk-shoh-pah
ball	to'wa'	toh'-wah'
belly	ittakoba'	it-tah-koh-bah'
dig	kolli	koh-le
eat	impa	im-pah
eyes	ishkin	ish-kin
fast	palhki	pulth-kee
food	impa'	im-pah'
friends	inkana'	ehn-kahn-nah'
good night	oklhili chokma	ohk-thlee-lee chog-mah
head	ishkobo'	ish-koh-boh'
hide	lohmi	loh-me

English	Chickasaw	Pronunciation
hungry	hopoba	hoh-poh-bah
legs	iyyi'	ee-yee'
nap	nosi	noh-see
ocean	okhata'	ohk-hut-ah'
ouch	alii	ah-lee
poke	baafa	bah-fah
sand	shinok	she-nuk
shell	hakshop	hak-shup
slow	salaa'si	sah-lah'-see
swim	yopi	yu-pee
tentacles	tashankchi'	tah-shunk-chee'
treat	naachampoli'	nah-chum-poh-lee'
water	oka'	oh-kah'

Hakshop
Shell

FUN FACT:

Long ago, Chickasaws used the fossilized shells of ancient bivalves, or mollusks, in pottery. The fossils were cleaned, crushed, and added to clay to "temper" it. The fossils made the pottery stronger and less likely to break when it was heated or cooled.

If fossils were fishes
And some of them are
And fishes were wishes
In an ocean of stars

And the moon in a dish
Was a dream come true
I'd wish on a fish
For a fossil or two

If wishes were starlight
Then beggars would sail
Through the heavenly night
On a trilobite's tail.